Walking with my Iguana

For Finch B M
For Ore Church Mice E B

Published by TROIKA

First published 2019

Troika Books Ltd
Well House, Green Lane, Ardleigh CO7 7PD
www.troikabooks.com

A CIP catalogue record
for this book is available
from the British Library

ISBN 978-1-909991-84-2

1 2 3 4 5 6 7 8 9 10

Printed in India

Walking with my Iguana

Brian Moses

illustrated by
Ed Boxall

troika

I'm walking, with my iguana.

I'm walking,
with my iguana.

When the temperature rises
to above eighty-five,
my iguana is looking
like he's coming alive.

So we make it to the beach,
my iguana and me,
then he sits on my shoulder
as we stroll by the sea . . .

And I'm walking, with my iguana.
I'm walking, with my iguana...

Well if anyone sees us
we're a big surprise,

my iguana and me
on our daily exercise,

till somebody phones
the local police

and says I have an alligator
tied to a leash.

When I'm walking, with my iguana.
I'm walking, with my iguana.

It's the spines on his back
that make him look grim,
but he just loves to be tickled
under his chin.

And I know that my iguana
is ready for bed
when he puts on his pyjamas
and lays down his sleepy (Yawn) head.

. . . piranha!

and my ...

chihuahua

and my ...

chinchilla,

with my gorilla

my caterpillar ...

and I'm walking,

with my iguana,

with my

Facts About Iguanas

- If you have an iguana as a pet and look after it properly, it can live for 12 to 15 years and up to 20 years in the wild.

- Iguanas like it hot. As it says in the book, 85º F (29.4º C) is ideal. They mostly live in rainforests.

- An iguana can use its tail to bash an enemy, and like most lizards it can lose its tail and grow another one.

- Iguanas can grow between 1.5 and 2 metres in length. They are the largest lizards in Central and South America.

- Iguanas eat fruit, flower buds and leaves.

- They have very strong teeth and powerful jaws.

- Female iguanas lay between 5 and 20 eggs which they bury in the sand in a sunny position. The mother then walks away, never to return. The baby iguanas are then on their own for three years before they are fully mature.

- Iguanas have a third eye on top of their heads that senses lightness, darkness and movement. They use this eye to watch out for enemies, particularly birds of prey.

- Iguanas are very good swimmers.

Hints on Performing 'Walking With My Iguana'

- Read the book to children and point out how the rhyme and the choral repetition give the poem a very strong rhythm.

- Read the book again with children joining in the choruses.

- Listen to Brian Moses read 'Walking With My Iguana' on the Poetry Archive: https://www.childrenspoetryarchive.org/poem/walking-my-iguana

- Show children how to drum along to the poem, either with drums, or using body percussion - clapping or tapping hands against thighs.

- Tap out the rhythm with them.

- Suggest that children find other creatures that they could walk with. Show them how they can substitute words and phrases while still keeping the rhythm.

*I'm walking
with my gorilla.
I'm walking
with my gorilla.*

*It's the teeth in his mouth
that make him look like he'll bite,
but he's sleepy all day
and most of the night.*

You can find another example – 'Walking With My Tortoise' plus background details as to what inspired Brian Moses to write 'Walking With My Iguana' here: http://brian-moses.blogspot.com/2012/10/walking-with-my-iguana-yes-iguanai.html

Have fun!

About the Author

BRIAN MOSES has been a professional children's poet since 1988. He has had over 200 books published including *Lost Magic* and *The Monster Sale* and edited anthologies such as *The Secret Lives of Teachers* and *Aliens Stole My Underpants*. His other books for Troika are *Beetle in the Bathroom* and *I Thought I Heard a Tree Sneeze: The very best of Brian Moses' Poems for Young Children*.

Brian also runs writing workshops and performs his own poetry and percussion shows. He has given over 3000 performances in schools, libraries, theatres and at festivals in UK and abroad. Brian is co-director of a nationwide able writers' scheme administered by Authors Abroad.

To find out more about Brian visit his website
www.brianmoses.co.uk

About the Illustrator

ED BOXALL is a childrens' poet, illustrator, musician, educator and performer.
He has written and illustrated many books, such as *Mr Trim and Miss Jumble* for Walker Books and *High In The Old Oak Tree* for his own Pearbox Press.
His first collection *Me and My Alien Friend: Cosmic Poems About Friendship* is published by Troika.
Ed performs his poems with a mix of spoken word and projections at schools, art centres and festivals. He lives in Hastings, a small town on the south coast of England.

To find out more about Ed visit his website
www.edboxall.com